Mission FARMERS' MARKET

written by
Marsha Qualey

illustrated by
Jessica Gibson

Raintree is an imprint of Capstone Global Library Limited, a company incorporated in England and Wales having its registered office at 264 Banbury Road, Oxford, OX2 7DY – Registered company number: 6695582

www.raintree.co.uk
myorders@raintree.co.uk

Edited by Helen Cox Cannons
Designed by Aruna Rangarajan
Original illustrations © Capstone Global Library Limited 2020
Illustrated by Jessica Gibson
Production by Kathy McColley
Originated by Capstone Global Library Limited
Printed and bound in India

ISBN 978 1 4747 9048 2

British Library Cataloguing in Publication Data
A full catalogue record for this book is available from the British Library.

CONTENTS

Meet
BEATRICE HONEY FLINN
(aka BUMBLE B.)

Hi, everyone!
I'm Beatrice Honey Flinn, but I prefer to be called Bumble B. You might think that is a strange name, but it makes a lot of sense. Let me explain:
1 My mum is a beekeeper, and my dad is an artist.
2 I tend to bumble a lot (which is a nice way of saying I'm a little clumsy).
3 My dad says I buzz through life with the persistence and confidence of a bee.
You mix all those reasons with a shortened version of Beatrice, and you get Bumble B. See? It all makes sense.
1+2+3=
BUMBLE B.

Mission

FARMERS' MARKET

LEMONS
30p/ea

Chapter 1

SWOOSH!

Bumble B. loved the farmers' market. She loved being outside. She loved helping her parents sell the honey from their honeybees.

She loved discovering new things to eat. She loved dancing to the music in the market square.

Bumble B. especially loved visiting Kayla's family at their garden stall. They had flowers and vegetables.

"Hi, Beatrice," said Kayla's grandma. "How are you today?"

Kayla's grandma was the only one who called Bumble B. by her full name. Bumble B. knew better than to argue with her.

"I'm great!" Bumble B. said. "Kayla invited me to help make flower bouquets."

"That's nice, dear," Kayla's grandma said. "Just make sure you get some work done."

"Don't you worry," Bumble B. said. "We are great workers!"

"Let's get started," Kayla said.

Grandma's van was parked behind the stall. The van was filled with vegetables and flowers. The girls crawled in.

"Each bouquet has five flowers. We use rubber bands to hold the flower stems together. It's easy," Kayla said.

Bumble B. watched Kayla make a bouquet. It did look easy. She started one of her own.

Bumble B. picked five flowers. She slipped a rubber band over the fingers of her right hand.

Then Bumble B. slowly opened her fingers. The rubber band stretched into a circle. Bigger... bigger... bigger...

Swoosh! The rubber band shot off her hand.

Kayla laughed. "You will get the hang of it."

Bumble B. tried again and again and again.

"Or maybe you won't," Kayla said, still laughing.

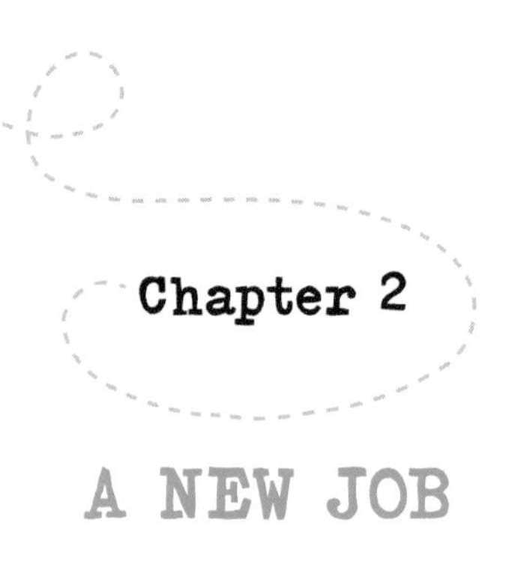

Chapter 2

A NEW JOB

When Grandma looked into the van, she didn't see many finished bouquets.

"You aren't getting much done. Please go and get water for the flowers. I will finish the bouquets," Grandma said.

On their way to the water tap, they saw an artist making funny portraits. The portraits were called caricatures.

"We have to get one together!" Bumble B. said.

“The queue is really long,” Kayla said.

“It will be worth the wait,” Bumble B. said. “Come on!”

When they returned with the fresh water, Grandma had finished the bouquets.

She was putting them out to sell. “What took you girls so long?”

“We got our pictures drawn,” Bumble B. said.

"Isn't it funny?" Kayla asked, holding up her picture.

"There is a time to work, and a time to play," Grandma said, not smiling.

She took Kayla's watering can. She filled the first flower bucket.

"I will fill the other one," said Bumble B.

She began pouring water. Just then, she smelled something wonderful.

She looked up to see a boy walking by with a bag of mini-doughnuts. She wished she had some doughnuts!

"Bumble B.! Stop!" Kayla shouted.

Bumble B. had watered

Grandma's shoe.

"Oh no!" Bumble B. yelled.

Kayla just giggled.

Grandma shook her head and took Bumble B.'s watering can. She finished pouring the water herself.

"I do make a lot of trouble," Bumble B. said.

Kayla hugged her. "You make a lot of fun!" she told her.

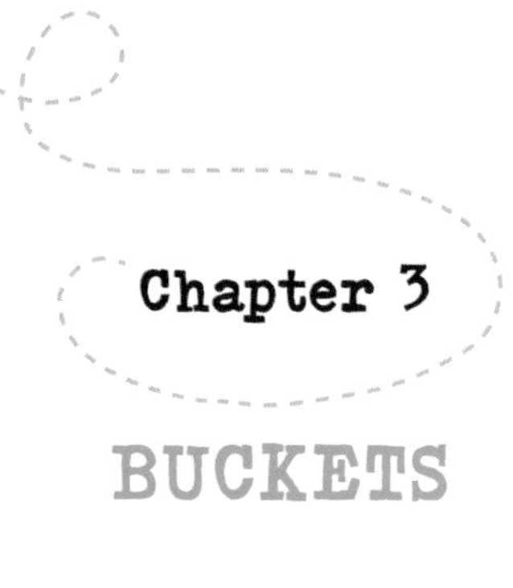

Chapter 3

BUCKETS

The bouquets were finally ready. A customer looked at one closely.

"This is beautiful," she said. "Where is your garden?"

While Kayla talked to her, Bumble B. studied the flowers.

They were beautiful, but

something was missing.

She whispered to her friend,

"I will be right back."

Bumble B. ran to her family's honey stall. She shouted hello to her mum and dad.

She crawled under the table and grabbed her rucksack. She found her colouring pens.

Bumble B. ran as fast as she could back to the garden stall.

"Flowers need insects," she told Kayla. She held up the pens. "Our mission is to draw them!"

"I was worried we weren't going to have time for a mission today," Kayla said.

"Don't be silly! There's always time for a mission," Bumble B. said.

They sat on the ground with the buckets. Bumble B. drew all of the shapes. Kayla coloured in the details.

"What are you girls doing with the flowers?" Grandma asked.

"We are making them better," Kayla said.

"Are you drawing on my buckets?" Grandma asked.

"It was my idea," Bumble B. said. "I'm sorry if I messed up again."

"We were just trying to help," Kayla said.

Grandma looked at each drawing. Then she smiled.

"It's a great idea, Beatrice. Honeybees need flowers, and flowers need honeybees," Grandmother said.

She pulled some money from her apron. "My hard workers should have a treat."

Bumble B. and Kayla thanked her, hugged her and held hands as they raced away.

It just happened to be double-scoop day at the ice cream van.

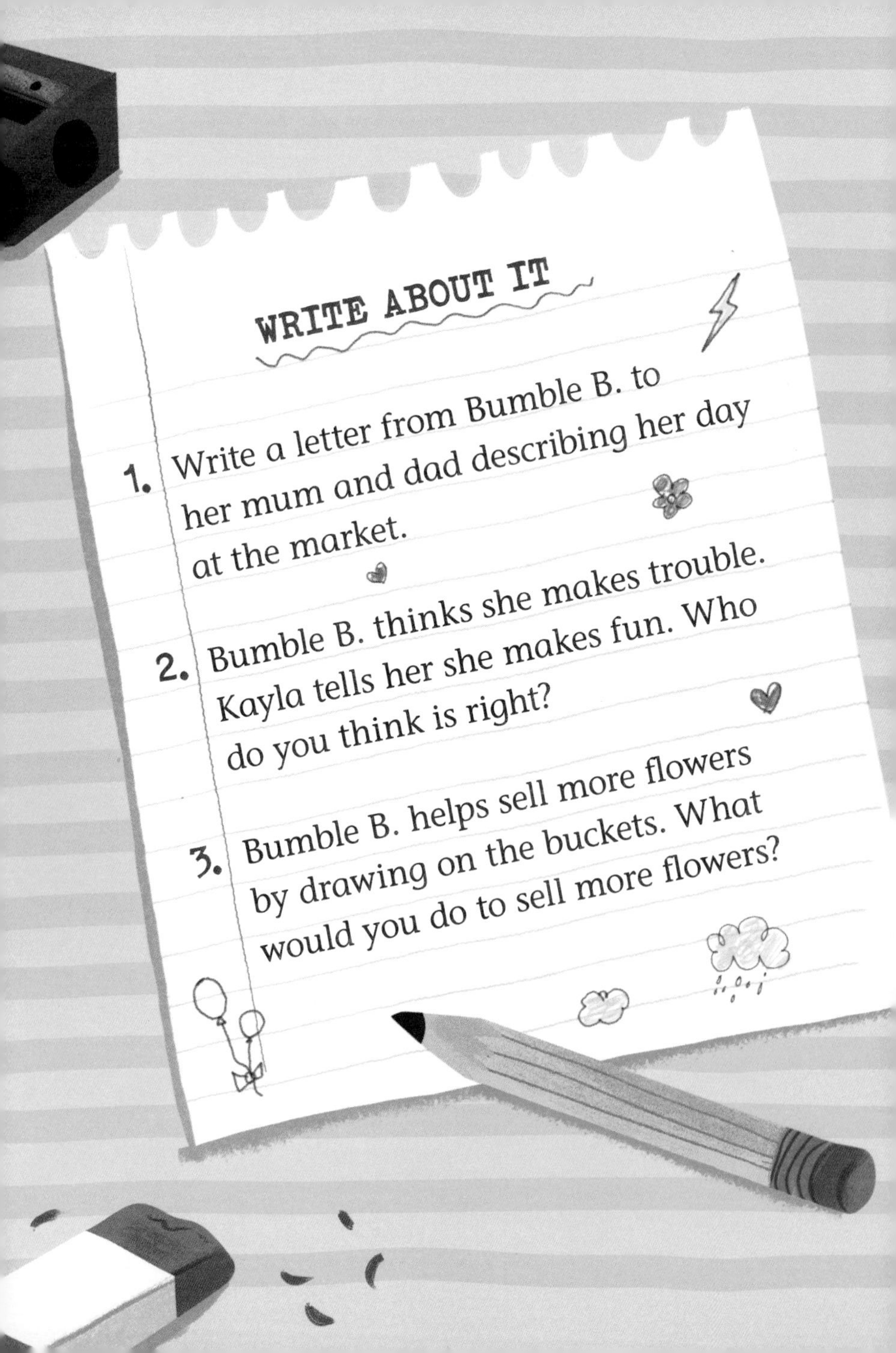

WRITE ABOUT IT

1. Write a letter from Bumble B. to her mum and dad describing her day at the market.
2. Bumble B. thinks she makes trouble. Kayla tells her she makes fun. Who do you think is right?
3. Bumble B. helps sell more flowers by drawing on the buckets. What would you do to sell more flowers?

TALK ABOUT IT

1. Bumble B. helps Kayla's grandma with her flower stall. Talk about a time you helped a relative.

2. Kayla's grandma is the only one who calls Bumble B. by her full name. Why do you think she does that?

3. Bumble B. likes to have a mission every day. Talk about a mission you could have.

GLOSSARY

bouquet bunch of picked or cut flowers

bumble act or speak in a clumsy way

caricature funny drawing of someone

customer person who buys goods or services

details small parts

farmers' market place where people sell fresh produce, flowers and other handmade items directly to customers

mission special job or task

ABOUT THE AUTHOR

Marsha Qualey is the author of many books for readers young and old. When she's not writing, she likes to read, go for walks by the river, ski in the winter, garden in the summer and play with her cats all year round. Like Bumble B., she has very good friends who make life fun.

ABOUT THE ILLUSTRATOR

Jessica Gibson is a freelance illustrator. With a pen and tablet by her side, Jessica loves creating adorable, whimsical and quirky illustrations, ready to brighten everyone's hearts.

FUN

Doesn't stop here!

You can read more books about Bumble B. and her friends.